PINOCCHIO

Pictures by T. IZAWA and S. HIJIKATA

GROSSET & DUNLAP • Publishers • NEW YORK
A NATIONAL GENERAL COMPANY

Many years ago there lived a lonely woodcarver named Geppetto, who made a poor living for himself in his little shop. He had no one at all with whom he could share his meals or his home, so one day he decided to carve a wooden puppet. Imagine his delight, upon finishing the puppet, to find that it could walk and talk! "I will call you Pinocchio," said the old man. Pinocchio was delighted, too. "Whee!" he cried. "I am a real boy! Look at me dance! Listen to me talk!"

Old Geppetto merely smiled—he knew that Pinocchio had much to learn before he would be a real boy.

"Now you must be off to school," he said one day. "This is all the money I have. Take it and buy yourself a schoolbook and then go directly to the schoolhouse. I will not have a dunce for a son."

Library of Congress Catalog Card Number: 77-157675
ISBN: 0-448-04274-6 (Trade Edition)
Illustrations Copyright © 1971 by Tadasu Izawa and Shigemi Hijikata
through management of Dairisha, Inc. Printed and bound in Japan
by Zokeisha Publications, Ltd., Roppongi, Minato-ku, Tokyo.

Pinocchio bought the book and set out for school. When he reached the village, he saw a crowd in front of a tent which was the Great Marionette Theatre. It cost four pennies to go in.

"I have no pennies at all," cried Pinocchio, aloud.

"I will give you four pennies for your schoolbook," offered a second-hand clothes man. Right then Pinocchio sold the book that had been bought with all the money old Geppetto had.

Leaving the theatre, Pinocchio saw a gaily painted coach, filled with laughing boys and pulled by donkeys wearing shoes. "Hop aboard!" cried the coachman. "We're off to Pleasure Island, where you can play all day to your heart's content. No school and no work!"

The foolish puppet thought that this was the best way to spend his time. As there was no room in the coach, he hopped on one of the donkeys.

Pleasure Island was exactly as the coachman had promised, filled with every delight. The time went by quickly, and Pinocchio enjoyed every minute. But imagine his horror one morning to discover two long donkey ears growing out of his head!

Then Pinocchio remembered the donkeys that had pulled the coach. They, too, must have been boys once! He thought of Geppetto and the sorrow he had caused the old man. "Oh, good fairy!" he cried. "I have been a foolish boy. Help me return to dear Geppetto and I will go to school and make him proud of me!"

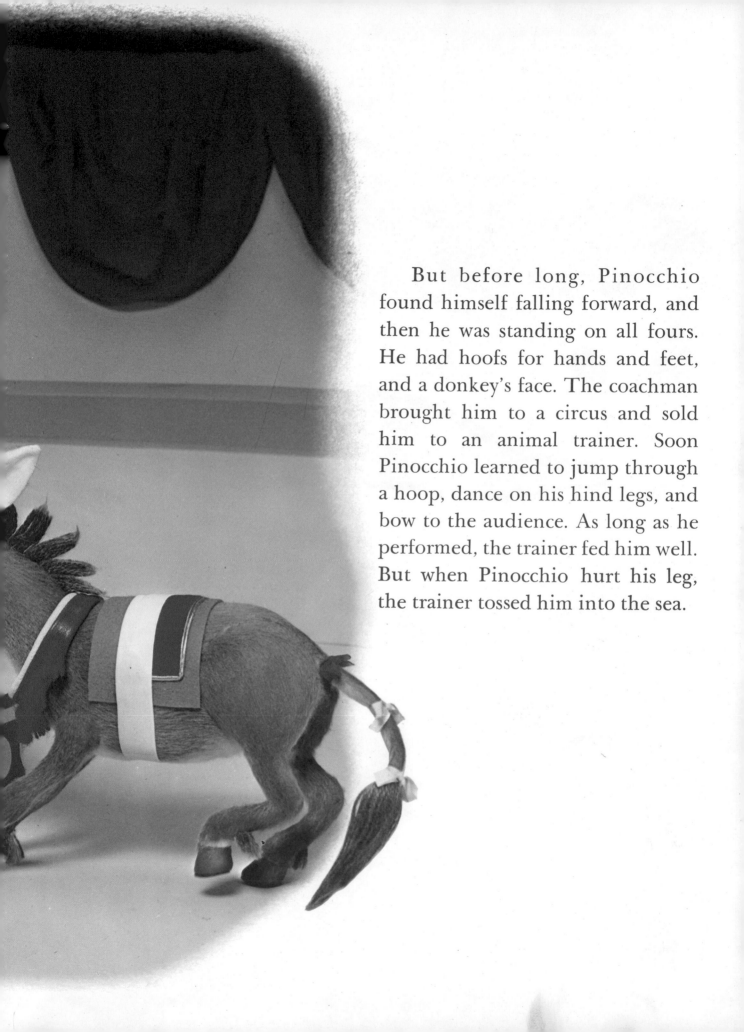

But before long, Pinocchio found himself falling forward, and then he was standing on all fours. He had hoofs for hands and feet, and a donkey's face. The coachman brought him to a circus and sold him to an animal trainer. Soon Pinocchio learned to jump through a hoop, dance on his hind legs, and bow to the audience. As long as he performed, the trainer fed him well. But when Pinocchio hurt his leg, the trainer tossed him into the sea.

In the sea the fish ate all the donkey flesh, but they could not eat the wood. When they finished, there was the wooden puppet! Pinocchio swam toward a rock where he saw a blue goat who reminded him of his beloved fairy godmother. But before he could reach the rock, a huge whale swam up behind him. It opened its giant mouth and swallowed Pinocchio in one gulp.

Pinocchio was terribly frightened, but then he began to feel his way in the darkness. At last he saw a faint light. As he approached it, he saw a candle on a small table and a small old man beside it. As soon as Pinocchio recognized him, he cried out, "Oh, my dear, dear Daddy! Oh, my good, good Geppetto!"

Hand in hand, Pinocchio and Geppetto climbed up the whale's throat and tip-toed along its tongue, which tickled the whale so that it sneezed. Pinocchio and Geppetto were blown out into the moonlit sea.

"I shall drown! I shall drown!" cried Geppetto. "I cannot swim."

"Climb on my back!" Pinocchio said, and when Geppetto had done so, the puppet swam quickly toward the shore.

Poor Geppetto was so cold and wet, he began to sneeze. When they reached shore, Pinocchio asked a farmer to put Geppetto to bed.

"Yes," said the farmer, "if you will work for me."

"Yes, yes," said Pinocchio. "My father must get well."

And so, Pinocchio worked from morning to night. There was no time for anything else.

When Geppetto became well enough, they returned to his house. Before they could greet each other, Pinocchio's good fairy appeared and put her hand on his shoulder. "Pinocchio," she whispered, "you have learned by now that you must work as well as play. I am sure you will be a good son to Geppetto."

She waved her wand and Pinocchio, the woodcarver's puppet, turned into a REAL live boy!